If I could ask GOD...

ANDY ROBB

Concordia Publishing House

Copyright © 2001 Angus Hudson Ltd/
Tim Dowley & Peter Wyart trading as Three's Company

Published by Concordia Publishing House
3558 S. Jefferson Avenue,
St. Louis, MO 63118-3968

ISBN 0 570 07181 X

Design by Peter Wyart

Worldwide coedition organised and produced by
Angus Hudson Ltd,
Concorde House, Grenville Place,
Mill Hill, London NW7 3SA, England
Tel: +44 (0) 20 8959 3668
Fax +44 (0) 20 8959 3678
E-mail: co-ed@angushudson.com

Printed in Singapore
1 2 3 4 5 6 7 8 9 10 10 09 08 07 06 05 04 03 02 01

Contents

Did Joseph's

Why were Joseph's brothers so mean to him?

What was Joseph's coat made of?

Did Joseph forgive his brothers?

Jacob loved his son Joseph more than all his other sons, so he gave him a special coat. Joseph's brothers were jealous. One day Joseph told them, "I had a dream that you bowed down to me." This made them so angry that the brothers sold Joseph as a slave. He was taken to Egypt, where his owner had him thrown into jail.

coat look cool?

Was Joseph always good at explaining dreams?

How did Joseph know what the dreams meant?

After a long time, Joseph was released because he could tell the ruler what his dreams meant. The ruler made Joseph his top official. Years later, Joseph's brothers came to Egypt looking for food. Joseph told them who he was. Jacob was reunited with his dear son, Joseph.
Genesis 37:1-36, 41:1-43, 45:3-28

What? questions would you ask

What did it smel

Were the birds in the ark in cages—or did they fly around?

What happened to the mess the animals made?

The people of the world had become very wicked. God decided to send a huge flood. A man named Noah had always been faithful to God. God said to Noah, "Build an ark big enough for your whole family and for every kind of animal."
When the ark was finished and everyone was onboard it started to rain. Soon floodwaters covered the whole earth.

like on Noah's ark?

Did Noah use a powerdrill to make the ark?

Did Noah and his family eat any of the animals in the ark?

After many weeks, the waters began to go down. At last the ark came to rest on a mountain. Noah and his family thanked God for His care. God sent a rainbow as a sign of His promise to never send another flood to destroy the whole world.
Genesis 6:9-8:21

What?
questions would you ask

Was manna like

Did the bush
burn up?

Where did all the
frogs go?

One day God spoke to Moses from a burning bush. "Go to the
Pharaoh of Egypt," He said. "Tell him to let My people go!"
Moses went—and Pharaoh refused. But Moses kept asking. God
sent terrible plagues—frogs, lice, and diseases—to the Egyptians.
At last Pharaoh gave in. Moses led the Israelite people out of
Egypt. When they reached the Red Sea, God made an amazing

breakfast cereal?

Did the fish stop at the wall of water?

What did God use to write the
Ten Commandments?

th through walls of water so they could escape from the
yptians.
the Israelites traveled through the desert to their new home
d, God provided food called manna. At Mount Sinai, God
ve Moses the Ten Commandments, written on tablets of stone.
odus 1:1-20:19

What? questions
would you
ask

Did the Israelites get dizzy

Was it like an earthquake when Jericho collapsed?

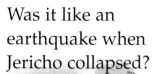

Did the people of Jericho think the Israelites were crazy?

God told Joshua, "I will help you capture the city of Jericho. March your army around the wall of the city every day for six days." Joshua did as God told him.

marching around Jericho?

Was it a long way around the city of Jericho?

What songs did the trumpeters play?

On the seventh day, Joshua and his army marched around the city seven times. The priests marched in front, blowing their trumpets. Suddenly everyone gave a loud shout, and the walls came tumbling down.
Joshua 6:1-20

What questions would you ask?

11

Was Samuel

How did Samuel know it was God speaking to him?

What did God's voice sound like?

Samuel grew up in the tabernacle. A priest named Eli took care of him. One night, Samuel heard a voice call his name. He ran to Eli and said, "Here I am!" But Eli said, "I didn't call you."

ust dreaming?

Did anyone else live in the tabernacle?

Did Samuel play games like we do today?

This happened two more times. Finally Eli realized it was God speaking to Samuel. The next time he heard God call, Samuel said, "Speak; your servant is listening." And God spoke to Samuel.
1 Samuel 3:1-10

What questions would you ask?

Did David do sling practice?

What made David so brave?

The Philistine army had gathered to fight the Israelites. Goliath, the Philistine champion, came out and roared, "I challenge any Israelite to fight me!" He was more than nine feet tall. They were all terrified. One day David came with food for his brothers who were in the army. He said, "I will fight Goliath."

like Superman?

Are there giants today?

What would have happened if David had run away?

He tried on the king's armor, but it was too heavy. So David went out to fight with a sling and five stones. Goliath laughed out loud when he saw him. David flung a stone at Goliath and he fell flat. Goliath died, and the Israelites thanked God for the victory.
1 Samuel 17:1-54

What? questions would you ask

Did Daniel pet
the lions?

Didn't the lions
like how Daniel
would have
tasted?

Daniel was captured and taken to faraway Babylon. But Daniel
became a favorite of Darius, king of Babylon. The king's
advisors were jealous of Daniel, so they tricked the king into
throwing Daniel into a den of lions because he prayed to God.

in the lions' den?

Did Daniel's enemies know they would end up in the lions' den?

Did King Darius start praying to God?

But God sent an angel to shut the lions' mouths. The next morning, King Darius discovered that Daniel was still alive. He freed him and praised God. The jealous advisors were thrown into the lions' den instead.
Daniel 6:1-28

What?
questions would you ask

Did Jonah give the big

Was it dark inside the big fish?

Did Jonah eat anything inside the fish?

God said to Jonah, "Go to Nineveh and tell the people to stop their wicked ways." But Jonah did not want to go, so he ran away to sea. God sent a terrible storm. Jonah knew he was to blame for the storm. He told the sailors to throw him overboard.
God sent a big fish to swallow Jonah. From inside the fish Jonah

fish a tummy ache?

What did Jonah do while he was inside the fish?

Why didn't the fish chew Jonah before he swallowed him?

...prayed, "Dear God, please save me!" After three days, the fish spit Jonah out onto dry land. Then Jonah did obey God. He went to Nineveh and preached God's message. The people repented and believed. Jonah 2:1-10

What? questions would you ask

Did Jesus get into trouble

How did Jesus know so much?

Were Jesus' mom and dad angry with Him for staying behind?

Every year Jesus' parents went to Jerusalem for the festival of the Passover. When Jesus was 12, He went along too. After the festival, Mary and Joseph left to go home. They didn't realize that Jesus wasn't with them. They thought He was with friends

for staying in the temple?

Did Jesus miss His parents?

Where did Jesus sleep in the temple?

and relatives. But Jesus had stayed in Jerusalem. Three days later Mary and Joseph found Jesus sitting in the temple. He was talking to the teachers. Everyone who heard Him was amazed at how much Jesus knew.
Luke 2:41-51

What? questions would you ask

Why did Jesus choose fishe

What happened to the fish they left behind?

Had Peter and Andrew met Jesus before He called them?

One day Jesus was walking beside the Sea of Galilee. He saw two brothers casting their fishing nets into the lake. They were named Simon (called Peter) and Andrew.

...en to be His disciples?

Did Jesus interview His disciples for their new job?

Were Peter and Andrew just fed up with fishing?

Jesus said, "Come, follow Me. I will make you fishers of men."
At once they left their nets and followed Jesus.
Matthew 4:18-20

What?
questions would you ask

One day a man named Jairus ran up to Jesus. He begged Jesus to come and heal his little girl, who was very ill. On their way, someone met them and said, "Don't waste Jesus' time. Your daughter is dead."

"Don't be afraid," said Jesus. "Just believe—and she will be healed."

girl to come back to life?

Why was Jairus' daughter dying?

Why was the girl hungry after she came back to life?

Did Jairus' daughter become famous?

After they got to the house, Jesus took the girl by the hand and said, "Get up, my child." The girl got up at once. The girl's parents were amazed.
Luke 8:40-42, 49-56

What?
questions would you ask

Was the boy
angry when Jesus
took his lunch?

What happened to
the 12 baskets of
leftovers?

One day a huge crowd of people—5000 men, not counting
women and children—followed Jesus into the country.
He taught them all day until they were very hungry. Jesus'
disciples did not know where to buy food for so many people.
One boy had five loaves of bread and two fish. "Make everyone

ourgers even bigger?

Did they eat the
fish raw—or did
God cook it first?

sit down," said Jesus. Then He gave thanks to God
for the food, and told His disciples to share with
everyone. Even after everyone had eaten as much as
they wanted, the disciples gathered 12 baskets of
leftovers.
John 6:1-13

What?
questions
would you
ask